For Sebastian
—E.C.

Clarion Books • a Houghton Mifflin Company imprint • 215 Park Avenue South, New York, NY 10003 • Copyright © 1991 by Eileen Christelow
Illustrations executed in gouache and pen and ink on Lanaquarelle hot-press watercolor paper • Text is 15-point Century Oldstyle • All rights reserved. • FIVE
LITTLE MONKEYS™, A FIVE LITTLE MONKEYS PICTURE BOOK™, and the monkey logo are trademarks of Houghton Mifflin Company. All rights
reserved. • For information about permission to reproduce selections from this book, write to Permissions, Houghton Mifflin Company, 215 Park Avenue
South, New York, NY 10003. • www.houghtonmifflinbooks.com • Printed in Malaysia. • The Library of Congress Catalog-in-Publication Data • Christelow,
Eileen. • Five little monkeys with nothing to do / written and illustrated by Eileen Christelow. • p. cm. • Summary: Five little monkeys are bored, but their
mother has them clean up the house for Grandma Bessie's visit. • ISBN 0-395-75830-0 • [1. Monkeys—Fiction.   2. House cleaning—Fiction.] I. Title
PZ7.C4523F1 1996 [E]—dc20 95-25873 CIP AC

CL ISBN-13: 978-0-395-75830-4   CL ISBN-10: 0-395-75830-0
PA ISBN-13: 978-0-618-04032-2   PA ISBN-10: 0-618-04032-3

TWP   15   14   13   12

Five Little Monkeys With Nothing to Do

Written and Illustrated by **Eileen Christelow**

Clarion Books/New York

It is summer. There is no school.
Five little monkeys tell their mama,
"We're bored. There is nothing to do!"
"Oh yes there is," says Mama.
"Grandma Bessie is coming for lunch,
and the house must be neat and clean.

"So . . . you can pick up your room."

9

Five little monkeys pick up and pick up and pick up . . .

. . . until everything is put away.

"Good job!" says Mama.
"But we're bored again,"
say five little monkeys.
"There is nothing to do!"
"Oh yes there is," says Mama.
"You can scrub the bathroom.
The house must be neat and clean
for Grandma Bessie."

So five little monkeys scrub and scrub and scrub until the bathroom shines.

"Good job!" says Mama.
    "But we're bored again,"
say five little monkeys.
"There is nothing to do!"
    "Oh yes there is," says Mama.
"You can beat the dirt out of these rugs.
The house must be neat and clean
for Grandma Bessie."

Five little monkeys beat and beat and beat the rugs until there is not a speck of dirt left.

"Good job!" says Mama.
"But we're bored again," say five little monkeys.
"There is nothing to do!"

"Oh yes there is," says Mama.
"You can pick some berries down by the swamp.
Grandma Bessie loves berries for dessert."

Five little monkeys run down
to the muddy, muddy swamp.

They pick and pick and pick berries
until Mama calls, "It's time to come home!"

Five little monkeys run inside
while Mama picks flowers.
    "Put the berries in the kitchen,"
calls Mama. "Wash your faces
and put on clean clothes."

25

Five little monkeys wash their faces . . .

. . . and they put on clean clothes.
"Grandma Bessie is here!" calls Mama.

Five little monkeys race outside.

They hug and kiss Grandma Bessie.

"We've been busy all day!" they say.
"We cleaned the house and picked berries
just for you!"

"I love berries," says Grandma Bessie.
"And I love a clean house, too!"

They all go inside.

"Oh my!" says Grandma Bessie.
"Oh dear!" says Mama.
"Oh no!" say five little monkeys.
"Who messed up our nice, clean house?"

"I can't imagine," says Mama.
"But whoever did has plenty to do!"

It's My Way

**Turning Bossy
into Flexible
and Assertive**

or the

HIGHWAY

Boys Town, Nebraska

ONE WAY

'JAKE' 'ANGUS' 'KIRBY'

Written by *Julia Cook*
Illustrated by *Kyle Merriman*

It's My Way or the Highway
Text and Illustrations Copyright © 2019 by Father Flanagan's Boys' Home
ISBN 978-1-944882-37-2

Published by the Boys Town Press
13603 Flanagan Blvd.
Boys Town, NE 68010

For a Boys Town Press catalog, call **1-800-282-6657**
or visit our website: **BoysTownPress.org**

Publisher's Cataloging-in-Publication Data

Names: Cook, Julia, 1964- author. | Merriman, Kyle, illustrator.

Title: It's my way or the highway : turning bossy into flexible and assertive / written by Julia Cook ; illustrated by Kyle Merriman.

Description: Boys Town, NE : Boys Town Press, [2019] | Series: The leader I'll be! | Audience: Grades K-6. | Summary: Cora June learns that there is a difference between being assertive and being bossy, and that she can be a leader and still be flexible. This is the first title in The Leader I'll Be! book series.--Publisher.

Identifiers: ISBN: 978-1-944882-37-2

Subjects: LCSH: Children--Life skills guides--Juvenile fiction. | Leadership in children--Juvenile fiction. | Assertiveness in children--Juvenile fiction. | Bossiness--Juvenile fiction. | Adaptability (Psychology) in children--Juvenile fiction. | Friendship in children--Juvenile fiction. | Interpersonal relations in children--Juvenile fiction. | Child psychology--Juvenile fiction. | CYAC: Conduct of life--Fiction. | Leadership--Fiction. | Assertiveness (Psychology)--Fiction. | Bossiness--Fiction. | Adaptability (Psychology)--Fiction. | Friendship--Fiction. | Interpersonal relations--Fiction. | Behavior--Fiction. | BISAC: JUVENILE FICTION / Social Themes / Self-Esteem & Self-Reliance. | JUVENILE FICTION / Social Themes / Values & Virtues. | JUVENILE FICTION / Social Themes / Friendship. | JUVENILE NONFICTION / Social Themes / Self-Esteem & Self-Reliance. | JUVENILE NONFICTION / Social Topics / Values & Virtues. | EDUCATION / Counseling / General. | SELF-HELP / Personal Growth / Success.

Classification: LCC: PZ7.C76982 I87 2019 | DDC: [E]--dc23

Printed in the United States
10 9 8 7 6 5 4 3 2

Boys Town Press is the publishing division of Boys Town, a national organization serving children and families.

My name is
Cora June.

People always say that
I am too **bossy,**
but I **don't** think I am.

*"I just know how
I want things to be.*

Don't do it that way. Listen to me!

We're playing this
because I say so.

It's **MY WAY** or the **HIGHWAY.**
You can't say **NO**!"

Yesterday at school, my teacher gave us a spelling worksheet that was **SUPER BORING.** I worked on it for a while, then stood up and said...

"I'm tired of doing this! Raise your hand if you want to go home."

Every single hand went up, except for my teacher's.

5

"Cora June, you need to sit down.
You are not the boss of this class!
If you can't figure out your worksheet,
please raise your hand and ask."

"But I don't want to do this,
and neither do they!
This class would be a lot more fun,
if you'd do things **MY WAY**!"

"Well, you can't always get what you want!

Someday, maybe you'll be a teacher. Then you can be the boss of your very own classroom. But right now, you are only the boss of you.

You need to be more **FLEXIBLE** and do your work."

7

At recess, I started a dodge ball game.
I picked the teams because...

"I just know how I want things to be.
Don't do it that way. Listen to me!
We're playing this because I say so.
It's MY WAY or the HIGHWAY. You can't say NO!"

"Cora June, you're being way too bossy again. You need to go to time-out and think about how you can be more **FLEXIBLE.**"

TIME

OUT

9

My best friend, Truman, came to my house after school to play.

"I get to go first.
You can't play with that!
Whatever you do,
don't pick up my cat!"

10

"I just know how I want things to be.
Don't do it that way. Listen to me!
We're playing this because I say so.
*It's **MY WAY** or the **HIGHWAY**. You can't say **NO**!"*

"You should be more
flexible, Cora June.
I'm going home!"

11

That night, Mom fixed bean soup for dinner.

"Bean soup? I'm not eating bean soup!
It gives me gas. It makes me toot!
You need to fix me something else,
like mac-and-cheese or a turkey melt!"

"Cora June,
we need to have a talk.
You think you're the boss,
but I'm sorry, you're not!

Your teacher called,
and told me about today.
It seems it's hard for you,
when you don't get your way.

You need to be more **FLEXIBLE!**"

"Yeah, I tried that. It doesn't help!"

14

"I just know how I want things to be...
but it seems like people won't listen to me!"

"Well, life just isn't all about you.
You have to think about other people, too.

You can't always get what you want."

15

"Cora June, you have everything you need to become a great leader, but none of that really matters if others don't want to follow you.

You need to use your **POWER OF** *Flexibility.*"

"But what does that even mean?"

"*YOU have a POWER inside your head,*
to help you say things a different way.
When you ask instead of tell,
people LISTEN to what you say!"

"Like today, when Truman was here. Instead of **TELLING HIM** what you wanted him to do, maybe you could have **ASKED HIM.** 'Hey, Truman, what game do you want to play?'"

"Your **POWER** of FLEXIBILITY helps you do things you don't want to do. It helps you learn how to listen to others... because life isn't all about you!"

ASSIGNMENT:
WRITE A FUNNY STORY USING THIS
WEEK'S SPELLING WORDS!

"Like at school today...

YOU are not in charge of your class, your teacher is!
It's her job to tell you what to do, and it's **YOUR** job to follow
instructions that will keep you safe and help you learn and grow."

"Oh, and always keep in mind, Cora June, you are in charge of your actions. Since I am your mom, and Daddy is your dad, it's our job to make sure we steer you down the right path. Someday, when you grow up, maybe you can be the mom and then you can be the boss. But right now, it isn't your turn!"

"Cora June, I love you so much.
I want you to be your best!
But without using your **POWER** of FLEXIBILITY,
your behavior is just a mess!"

Maybe Mom is right.

At school, I did everything my teacher asked.
And I didn't try to be the boss.

At recess, I let other kids pick the teams...
even though we lost.

Truman came over after school again,
and I let him choose what to do.

I even ate leftover bean soup,
and I didn't even say

'EWWWWW!''

I used my **POWER** OF *Flexibility* the **WHOLE** entire day.

It helped me realize
life's still OK...
when I don't get my way.

29

But I **still** like to be
the boss **sometimes.**

Some children are natural leaders, and the last thing you want to do is stifle their leadership abilities.

It's crucial that kids understand that being a leader doesn't mean they are free to boss anyone around in any situation. Here are some strategies to help young people become more aware of how their actions are perceived by others and how to encourage calm, assertive leadership skills rather than aggressive, domineering behaviors.

1. Explain the differences between bossiness and assertiveness. **Bossiness** is being fond of giving orders and being domineering, regardless of how it makes others feel. **Assertiveness** is having or showing a confident, take-charge personality while being aware of how your actions might affect others. *Helpful hint: You can't lead if no one follows.*

2. Be a good role model by communicating your own flexibility when things aren't going your way. Use those moments to reinforce leadership skills in others.

3. Set appropriate boundaries and, when crossed, **always follow through** with appropriate consequences. Kids must learn that inappropriate actions have consequences, or they will do whatever they want to whomever they want whenever they want!

4. Always praise children when they are polite and kind to others. Being kind and assertive are not mutually exclusive.

5. Teach children to use their **POWER of FLEXIBILITY.** *"You won't always get what you want, so try to be more flexible and you'll get through it!"*

6. Use a private signal system (i.e., pulling your ear) to warn a child when he's being bossy. Allow him to self-correct the situation. Remember, self-awareness is key.

7. When you hear a child being bossy, help her rephrase the bossy comments in a way that is more assertive and empathetic. *Helpful hint: Hold a mirror up to the child's face and ask her to repeat the bossy comments. Then ask, "Would you like it if somebody spoke that way to you? Let's see if we can figure out a nicer, less aggressive way to communicate."*

8. When power struggles arise, offer choices with limits. For example, "You get to choose. Are you going to brush your teeth before your story or after your story?"

9. Whether a parent or teacher, you are the boss. Respect your power and how you use it.

For more parenting information, visit **boystown.org/parenting.**

BOYS TOWN®
Saving Children   Healing Families

Boys Town Press Books by Julia Cook

Kid-friendly titles to teach social skills

The Leader I'll Be! teaches children how to use collaboration, creativity and compromise to influence others.

978-1-944882-37-2

978-1-944882-44-0

Responsible ME!

A book series that delivers a powerful message about accountability and honesty.

978-1-934490-30-3

978-1-934490-80-8

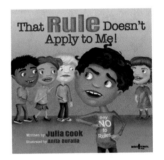
978-1-934490-98-3

CHEATERS Never Prosper
978-1-944882-08-2

OTHER TITLES: Baditude!, The Procrastinator

NEW TITLES

UNIQUELY WIRED
A Story about Autism and Its Gifts
Written by Julia Cook
Illustrated by Anita DuFalla

RUMOR HAS IT...
Illustrated by ...MERRIMAN
Written by JULIA COOK

Building RELATIONSHIPS
A book series to help kids get along.

Making Friends Is an Art!
Cliques Just Don't Make Cents
Tease Monster
Peer Pressure Gauge
Hygiene...You Stink!
I Want to Be the Only Dog
The Judgmental Flower
Table Talk
Rumor Has It...

COMMUNICATE with Confidence
A book series to help kids master the art of communicating.

Well, I Can Top That!
Decibella
Gas Happens!
The Technology Tail

BEST ME! I Can Be
Winner of the Mom's Choice Award!

The Worst Day of My Life Ever!
el PEOR día de TODA mi vida
I Just Don't Like the Sound of NO!
¡No me gusta cómo se oye NO!
Sorry, I Forgot to Ask!
I Just Want to Do It My Way!
Teamwork Isn't My Thing, and
I Don't Like to Share!
Thanks for the Feedback... (I Think!)
I Can't Believe You Said That!